LoVE
MeMa & PoPPY

D1232001

Angels Watchin'

Written by A. Shelton Rollins
Illustrated by Pamela Carthorn

LIFT EVERY VOICE / CHICAGO

DEDICATIONS:

To Diandra, my inspiration, and to Grandma Mattie, Grandma Shelton, Granny, Gran, Grandma Josie, and all the grandmothers who love their grandchildren.

— A. Shelton Rollins

To my Lord Jesus Christ, for His infinite love and extraordinary patience toward me. And to my husband, Maliek, for being Christlike in reflecting that same love and patience of the Lord.

— Pamela Carthorn

LIFT EVERY VOICE, A Division of Moody Publishers, 820 N. LaSalle Boulevard, Chicago, IL 60610-3284

First published in 2003 by Lift Every Voice, Copyright © A. Shelton Rollins, 2003.
Illustrations copyright © Pamela Carthorn, 2003. All rights reserved.

ISBN 0-8024-2921-1

Printed in Italy by L.E.G.O. SpA

Scripture taken from the NEW AMERICAN STANDARD BIBLE®,

Copyright © The Lockman Foundation 1960, 1962, 1963, 1968, 1971, 1972, 1973, 1975, 1977, 1995. Used by permission.

Terra was like most seven-year-old girls. Sometimes she liked to play with her friends, and sometimes she liked to be alone.

Sometimes she was happy, and sometimes she was sad.

Sometimes she felt like she could do anything, and sometimes she was afraid.

Mostly, Terra was afraid at night. When the lights were low, the everyday things didn't seem so everyday.

And in her mind, she imagined all kinds of scary things.

Her momma and daddy tried to help. "God loves you," Momma would say gently. "And He watches over you all the time."

"Pray, and think about God and good things," said Daddy, "And remember, your momma and I are here."

Terra listened. And she prayed. But the fear stayed.

4

That Fourth of July, Grandma Ruthie came to visit.

Terra loved her easy smile, her dancing eyes, and the way her voice sang when she called Terra "Baby."

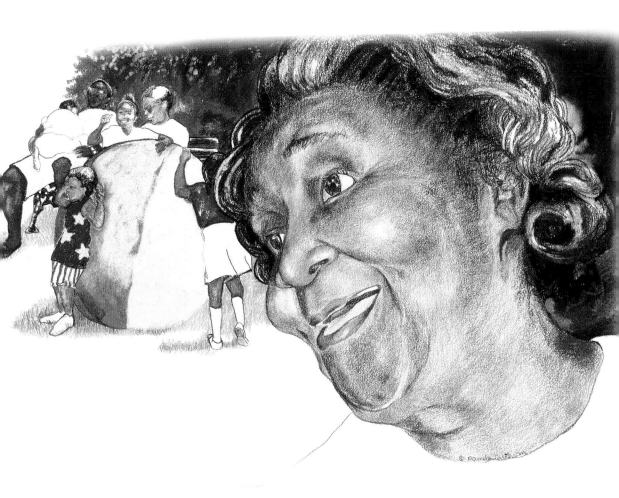

Terra loved the hugs, the tickles, and even the "How's my Sugar?" pinches she gave.

Terra loved Grandma Ruthie.

But even after the church picnic and fireworks, even with Grandma Ruthie in the house, Terra lay in her bed that night, afraid.

Momma came and went. Daddy did too. Then Grandma Ruthie entered the room.

"Hi, Baby," Grandma whispered sweetly. "I heard you were havin' some trouble sleepin'."

Terra only nodded her head, too embarrassed to speak a yes.

"Ain't nothin' to be ashamed of," said Grandma Ruthie with a huff. "Anybody can be afraid. What you have to remember—what you have to believe—is that you are never alone."

Grandma sat down next to Terra on the bed and squeezed Terra's hand in her own round one. "Let me tell you a story," she said, wrapping the quilt around them.

"This story is older than me and you," Grandma began. "This story is about a girl named Elizabeth. Now, Elizabeth was a slave girl. And people from Africa who were made to be slaves—well, they were treated pretty bad.

They didn't have much, and they worked real hard. They couldn't bake cookies for fun the way we do, or sit at a softball game.

They belonged to someone, the way a horse belongs to a farmer."

"Why?" Terra whispered.

"Because when people don't listen to God, they do bad things," said Grandma.

"That's the only way to explain what would make a person keep another person and treat them bad for their whole life. But do you know what? Even when people want to hurt you, God can make something good out of it."

"What do you mean?" asked Terra.

"Well," continued Grandma, using the quilt as her storyboard, "one thing that happened to slaves sometimes was that they would be sold, the way a farmer might sell that horse he owns. Most slave families weren't allowed to stay together. And the day came when Elizabeth had to be sold."

"Away from her parents?" asked Terra, suddenly feeling Elizabeth's fear.

"Away from her parents," said Grandma Ruthie. "And she was afraid. There was nothing Elizabeth's mother or father could do to stop her from going, but they gave Elizabeth a special gift."

"What gift?" Terra asked.

Grandma leaned closer to Terra before going on. "Something to remember from the Bible. You know, even though some slave owners tried to use the Bible to make slaves weak, God used that same Bible to make slaves strong. Their songs and their lives proved they understood what the Bible said about a lot of things, including angels," said Grandma Ruthie.

"Angels?" quizzed Terra.

"Yes," said Grandma. "Did you know you have your own angel?"

Terra nodded a yes, but Grandma frowned. "No, Baby," she said, shaking her head. "Do you know it? Do you believe it?"

Terra didn't answer. So Grandma Ruthie continued. "Well, Elizabeth didn't believe it either—until she had to. And she had to when her owner sold her. A wagon came that day, and there were whispers around the farm. Elizabeth's mother called Elizabeth into their one-room shack."

"Baby,' said Elizabeth's mother, 'now, you're going somewhere that I can't go. But God is with you. He said He will never leave you, and you know He never lies. And your own angel will be there for you, too. God has special angels to watch over children—and to help us when we are older.'

Then her mother sang this song:

'All night, all day
Angels watchin' over me, my Lord.
All night, all day
The angels are watchin' over me'."

"'Baby, you are never alone'," said Elizabeth's mother.

'And one day, because you and your papa and I have Jesus in our hearts, we'll be together again.'

Elizabeth and her mother prayed, and suddenly Elizabeth didn't feel alone."

"The Bible says that angels sometimes appear as humans and, in Elizabeth's mind, her angel had a gown brighter than new snow.

She had gentle eyes and a face the color of dark brown sugar.

Elizabeth had to leave her parents that day, but she never forgot about her angel.

That angel reminded her day and night of God's care, and so did the song.

It helped Elizabeth to remember that no matter how bad life was—and it was bad many times—she had a Friend that no one, not even her slave owner, could take from her.

A Friend that loved her enough to give her a special angel."

The room was quiet, and Terra thought about her angel.

In her mind, she could see her angel with her when she was with her friends and when she was alone.

She could see her angel with her when she was happy and when she was sad.

And she could see her angel with her when she was afraid.

Suddenly, Terra felt at peace and smiled. "Thank you, Grandma," said Terra.

Then Grandma Ruthie smiled—the kind of smile you smile when you get a special gift. "You're welcome, Baby," she said, and she pinched Terra's cheek.

As Grandma left, Terra closed her eyes.

She imagined her angel's glowing presence watching over her as she slept, and she whispered, softly,

All night, all day
Angels watchin' over me, my Lord.
All night, all day
The angels are watchin' over me.

Scriptures

"I will never desert you, nor will I ever forsake you" (Hebrews 13:5).

" . . . it is impossible for God to lie..." (Hebrews 6:18).

"See that you do not despise one of these little ones, for I say to you that their angels in heaven continually behold the face of My Father who is in heaven" (Matthew 18:10).

"The angel of the Lord encamps around those who fear Him" (Psalm 34:7).